Ozzie is the laziest owl in the world. Mother Owl is determined to make him fly but he can't be bothered. How can he get to the ground without flying? Ozzie devises a very clever plan, involving all the farm animals, but it's still Mother Owl who has the last laugh!

ISBN 1-84506-062-8

9 781845 060626 > £5.99

www.littletigerpress.com

This Little Tiger book belongs to:

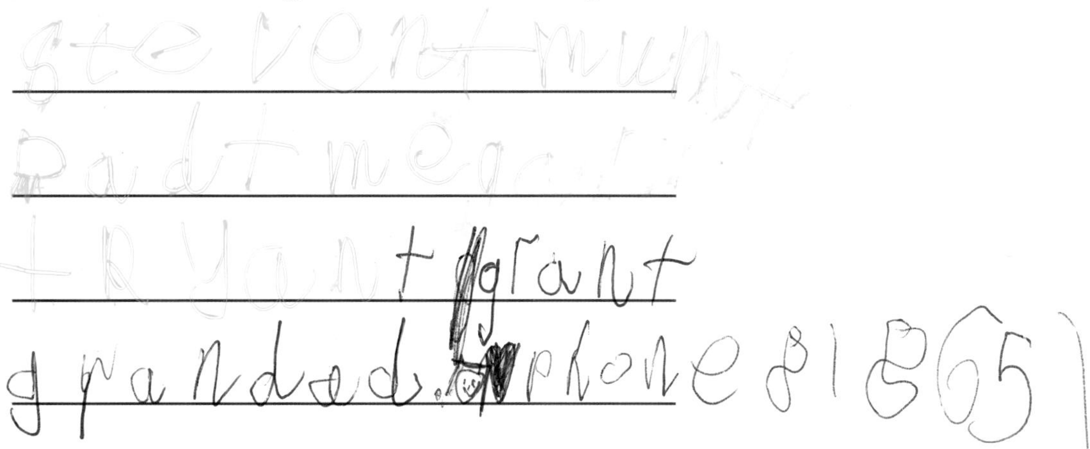

In Memory of Michael Murphy
~ M.C.

For Mum & Dad
~ G.W.

LITTLE TIGER PRESS
An imprint of Magi Publications
1 The Coda Centre, 189 Munster Road, London SW6 6AW
www.littletigerpress.com
First published in Great Britain 1994
This edition published 2004

A CIP catalogue record for this book is available from the British Library
 • ISBN 1 84506 062 8 • Printed in China
3 5 7 9 10 8 6 4 2

Lazy Ozzie

Michael Coleman

Illustrated by

Gwyneth Williamson

Little Tiger Press

London

Ozzie was a very lazy owl.

"It's time you tried to fly," said Mother Owl one day.

But Ozzie just said, "Oh, do I have to?"

Ozzie didn't fancy flying one little bit. It seemed much too much hard work, all that wing-flapping. He just wanted to sit around all day. "I'm practising being wise," he said.

"Well, I want you to fly,"
said Mother Owl sternly.
"Now, I'm going off to look
for some food. And if you *are* wise,
you will be on the ground by the time I come back!"

Ozzie thought hard.
If he was wise, then he should be able to think of a way of getting down to the ground without flying.
Suddenly he noticed the horse who lived in their barn. The horse's head came up almost as high as the beam Ozzie was sitting on.
Ozzie had an idea . . .

"Help, help!" he yelled.
"What's the matter
with you, then?"
said the high horse.

"It's an emergency!" shouted Ozzie, jumping on to the high horse's back. "Take me to the cowshed!"

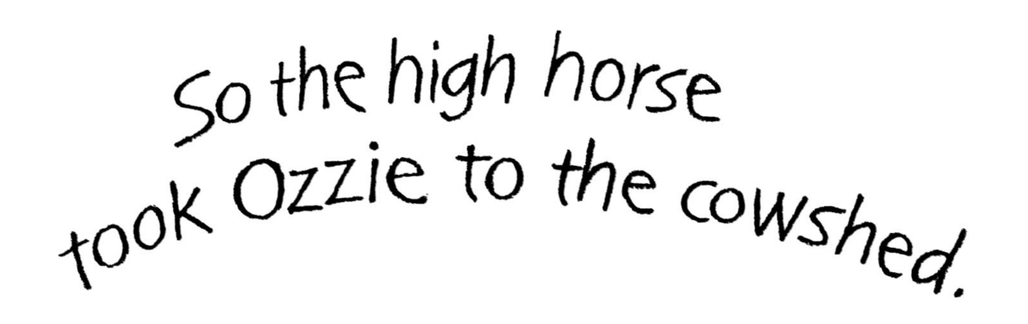

So the high horse
took Ozzie to the cowshed.

In the cowshed there lived a cow who wasn't quite as high as the high horse.

"It's an emergency!" cried Ozzie, jumping on to the not-quite-so-high cow's back. "Take me to the pigsty!"

So the high horse and
the not-quite-so-high cow
took Ozzie to
the pigsty.

In the pigsty there lived a big pig.
"It's an emergency!" cried Ozzie, jumping on to the big pig's back. "Take me to the farmyard!"

So the high horse,
the not-quite-so-high cow
and the big pig took Ozzie
to the farmyard.

In the farmyard there lived a sheepdog.
The sheepdog wasn't as tall as the big pig.
He was a short sheepdog.
"It's an emergency!" cried Ozzie,
jumping on to the short sheepdog's back.
"Take me to the big field!"

So the high horse,
the not-quite-so-high cow,
the big pig and the short
sheepdog took Ozzie to
the big field.

In the big field there lived a little lamb.

"It's an emergency!" cried Ozzie, jumping on to the little lamb's back.

"Take me to the duck pond!"

So the high horse, the not-quite-so-high cow, the big pig, the short sheepdog and the little lamb took Ozzie to the duck pond.

In the duck pond there lived a diddy duck.
"It's an emergency!" cried Ozzie, jumping on to the diddy duck's back. "Take me to the barn!"

So the high horse, the not-quite-so-high cow,
the big pig, the short sheepdog,
the little lamb and the diddy duck
took Ozzie back to the barn...

As soon as they got there, Ozzie hopped from the diddy duck's back down to the ground.
He'd done it!
Now that's what you call being wise, he told himself!

"So where's the emergency?" asked the high horse.
"Ah," said Ozzie. "I was only joking.
What a hoot, eh?"

The high horse, the not-quite-so-high cow,
the big pig, the short sheepdog, the little lamb
and the diddy duck weren't amused.
They went away grumbling.
But Ozzie was pleased. His plan had worked.
He was pretty wise already.

"I flew all the way down,"
he said to Mother Owl
when she came back.

Mother Owl gave a big smile.
"Well done, son," she said.
Ozzie thought she was
pleased with him . . .

. . . but he didn’t know
she’d been watching
all the time.
“Now let me see you
fly back up again,” said
Mother Owl.

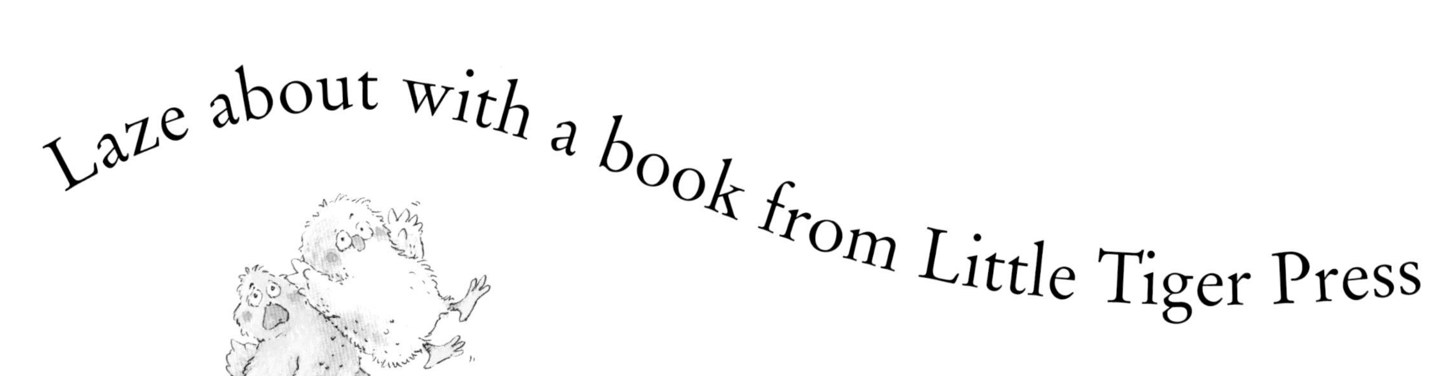

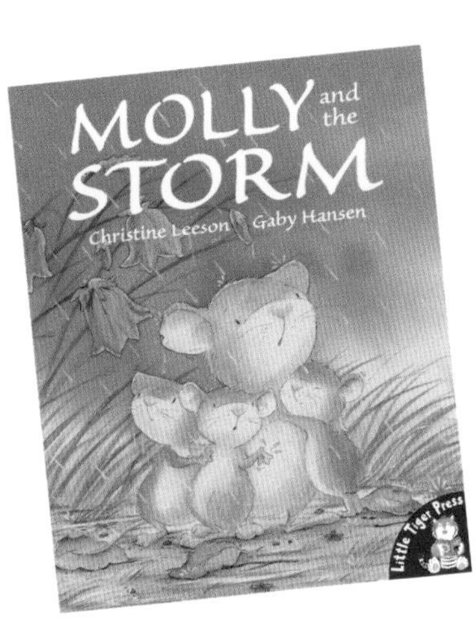

Dilly Duckling
By Claire Freedman
Illustrated by Jane Chapman
Little Tiger Press

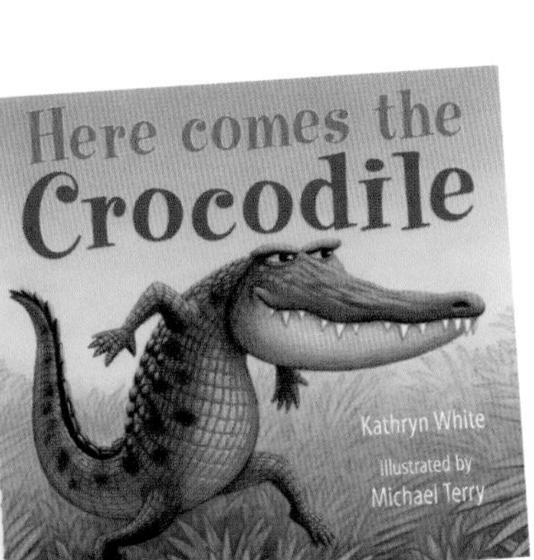

For information regarding any of the above titles or for our catalogue, please contact us:
Little Tiger Press, 1 The Coda Centre,
189 Munster Road, London SW6 6AW
Tel: 020 7385 6333 Fax: 020 7385 7333
Email: info@littletiger.co.uk
www.littletigerpress.com